Nana Upstairs &
Nana Downstairs

Nana Upstairs & Nana Downstairs

written and illustrated by
Tomie dePaola

G. P. Putnam's Sons
New York

For all my family, especially those who remember
Honorah O'Rourke Mock and Alice Mock Downey—
Nana Upstairs and Nana Downstairs

Text copyright © 1973 by Tomie dePaola.
Illustrations copyright © 1998, 1973 by Tomie dePaola.
All rights reserved. This book, or parts thereof, may not be reproduced
in any form without permission in writing from the publisher.
G. P. Putnam's Sons, a division of The Putnam & Grosset Group,
200 Madison Avenue, New York, NY 10016.
G. P. Putnam's Sons, Reg. U.S. Pat. & Tm. Off.
Artwork based on the 1973 edition published by G. P. Putnam's Sons.
Published simultaneously in Canada.
Printed in Hong Kong by South China Printing Co. (1988) Ltd.
Book design by Patrick Collins and Donna Mark.
Text set in Century Old Style.
Library of Congress Cataloging-in-Publication Data
dePaola, Tomie. Nana Upstairs & Nana Downstairs /
story and illustrations by Tomie dePaola   p. cm.
Summary: Four-year-old Tommy enjoys his relationship with both
his grandmother and great-grandmother, but eventually
learns to face their inevitable death.
[1. Grandmothers—Fiction. 2. Great-grandmothers—Fiction.
3. Old age—Fiction. 4. Death—Fiction.] I. Title.
PZ7.D439Nan 1997 [E]—dc20 96-31908 CIP AC
ISBN 0-399-23108-0
1 3 5 7 9 10 8 6 4 2
FIRST IMPRESSION

When Tommy was a little boy, he had a grandmother and a great-grandmother.

He loved both of them very much.

He and his family would go to visit every Sunday afternoon. His grandmother always seemed to be standing by the big black stove in the kitchen.

His great-grandmother was always in bed upstairs because she was ninety-four years old.

So Tommy called them Nana Downstairs and Nana Upstairs.

Almost every Sunday was the same. Tommy would run into the house, say hello to his Grandfather Tom and Nana Downstairs, and then go up the back stairway to the bedroom where Nana Upstairs was.

"Get some candy," Nana Upstairs would say. And he would open the lid of the sewing box on the dresser, and there would be candy mints.

Once Nana Downstairs came into the bedroom and helped
Nana Upstairs to the big Morris chair and tied her in so she
wouldn't fall out.

"Why will Nana Upstairs fall out?" Tommy asked.
"Because she is ninety-four years old," Nana Downstairs said.
"I'm four years old," Tommy said. "Tie me in a chair too!"

So every Sunday, after he found the candy mints in the sewing box on the dresser, Nana Downstairs would come up the back stairway and tie Nana Upstairs and Tommy in their chairs, and then they would eat their candy and talk.

Nana Upstairs told him about the "Little People."

"Watch out for the fresh one with the hat with the red feather in it. He plays with matches," she said.

"I will," said Tommy.

"There he is!" she said. "Over by the brush and comb. See him?"

Tommy nodded.

When Nana Downstairs had finished her work by the big black stove and baked a cake to eat before Tommy went home, she would come back upstairs.

"Now," Nana Downstairs would say as she untied Tommy from his chair. "We must all take our naps."

After their naps, Nana Downstairs would comb out Nana
Upstairs' beautiful silver-white hair.

Then Nana Downstairs would comb and brush her own hair.

"Now make the 'cow's tail'!" Tommy would say.
And she would twist her hair and pin it up on top of her head.

One time Tommy's older brother came into the bedroom and saw Nana Upstairs with her hair all down around her shoulders, and he ran away.

"She looks like a witch!" he said.

"She does *not*!" Tommy said. "She's beautiful."

"Time for ice cream!" shouted Grandfather Tom. And Tommy and his brother went with him, and sometimes their father and their Uncle Charles, down to the ice-cream store.

When they got back, it was time for Nana Upstairs to have a snack, and Tommy would help carry the tray of milk and crackers up the back stairway.

Once Tommy's father took movies of the whole family.
He took movies of Nana Downstairs and Nana Upstairs.
And Tommy stood in the middle.

One morning when Tommy woke up at his own house, his mother came in to talk to him.

"Nana Upstairs died last night," she said.

"What's 'died'?" Tommy asked.

"'Died' means that Nana Upstairs won't be here anymore," Mother answered.

They went to Tom and Nana Downstairs' house, even though it wasn't Sunday.

Tommy ran up the back stairway before he'd even said hello. He ran into Nana Upstairs' room.

The bed was empty.

Tommy began to cry.

"Won't she ever come back?" he asked.

"No, dear," Mother said softly. "Except in your memory. She will come back in your memory whenever you think about her."

From then on he called Nana Downstairs just plain Nana.

A few nights later, Tommy woke up and looked out his bedroom window at the stars.

All of a sudden, a star fell through the sky. He got up and ran to his mother and father's bedroom.

"I just saw a falling star," he said.
"Perhaps that was a kiss from Nana Upstairs," said Mother.

A long time later, when Tommy had grown up, Nana Downstairs was old and in bed just like Nana Upstairs. Then she died too.

And one night, when he looked out his bedroom window, Tommy saw another star fall gently through the sky.

Now you are both Nana Upstairs, he thought.

This book is a true story.

I still consider it a wonderful experience and privilege that I knew not only two grandmothers and one grandfather but my Irish great-grandmother as well. The Irish side of my family (I'm half Irish and half Italian) lived nearby, so we saw them weekly, and I spent many hours with Nana Upstairs, tied into the adjoining chair, eating candy mints. She was my very best friend when I was four years old.

The original edition of this book, written in 1972 and published in 1973, was illustrated in three colors—black, pink, and ochre. It was not easy to re-illustrate the book in full color. It was hardly a matter of "colorizing" or coloring in. My drawing style has changed subtly over time, so twenty-five years later I have approached *Nana Upstairs & Nana Downstairs* as a completely new book. It was important for me to retain the nostalgic feeling of the original, and I did this mostly with the use of soft color. Creating this art was as emotional an experience for me now as it was then.

So here's to Honorah O'Rourke Mock and Alice Mock Downey— Nana Upstairs and Nana Downstairs.

T. DEP.
NH, 1998